D1712348

PEEK-A-BOO MAGIC

To Nathan

Pat Bacon

1995

Library of Congress-in-Publication Data
Bagley, Patrick.
Peek-a-boo Magic / written and illustrated by Pat Bagley.
p.   cm.
Secret decoder included.
Summary: Using a colored decoder, the reader joins several children
as they try to find different animals hiding in the illustrations.
ISBN 1-8885628-00-5
1. Toy and movable books—Specimens.
[1. Animals—Fiction. 2. Stories in rhyme.
3. Toy and movable books.] I. Title.
PZ8.3.B14Pe 1995
[E] dc20   95-15050
CIP   AC

Printed and bound in the United States

If you lose your looking glass send $1.95 check or money order to:
Buckaroo Books, 2533 North Carson Street, Suite 1544
Carson City, Nevada 89706

PEEK-A-BOO MAGIC

Written and Illustrated
by Pat Bagley

BUCKAROO BOOKS

Can you find. . .

Peek-a-boo fox

Peek-a-boo Rex

Peek-a-boo otter

Peek-a-moo cow

Peek-a-boo teddy

Peek-a-mew cat

Peek-a-boo elephant

Peek-a-boo gator

Peek-a-boo monkey

Peek-a-boo pig

Peek-a-boo roo

Peek-a-boo sheep

Cats enjoy napping,

Dogs prefer walks,

But for a romp in the country
Chase a peek-a-boo fox.

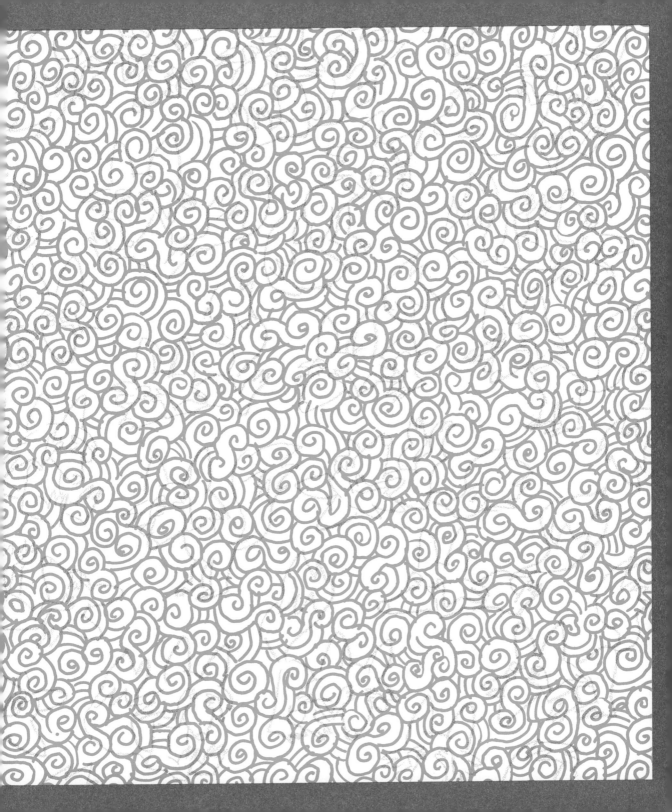

Teeth that bite
And claws that vex,

Can you find
A peek-a-boo Rex?

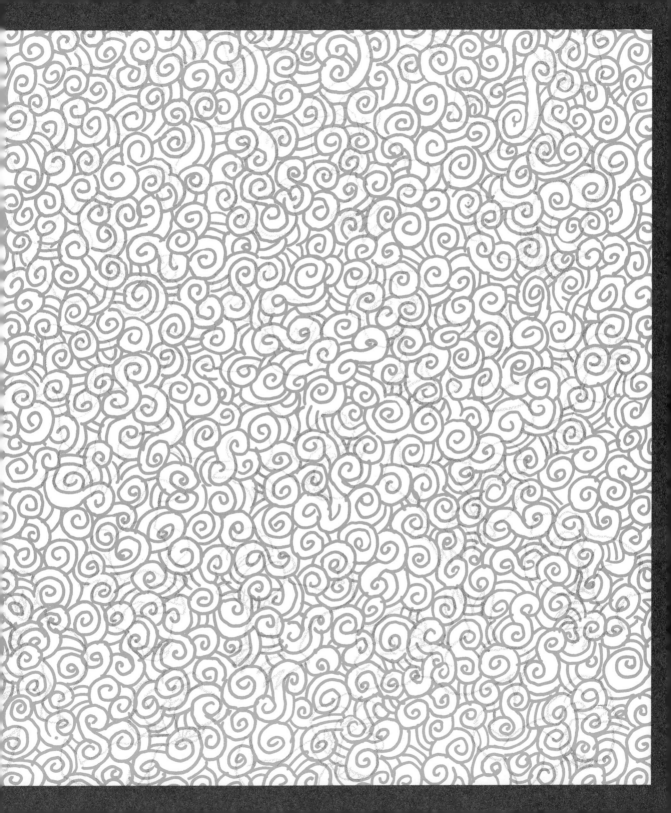

Want to stay dry?
Keep out of the water—
Cause that's where you'll find
A peek-a-boo otter.

Shoot off like a rocket!
Zing, zang, zow!
Look! In the sky—
It's a peek-a-boo cow!

They come in grizzly, brown, and teddy
And their manners are so sweet,
But if one should call you "honey"
Don't end up a peek-a-boo treat.

Mice in front
And more in back,

Time to find
A peek-a-mew cat.

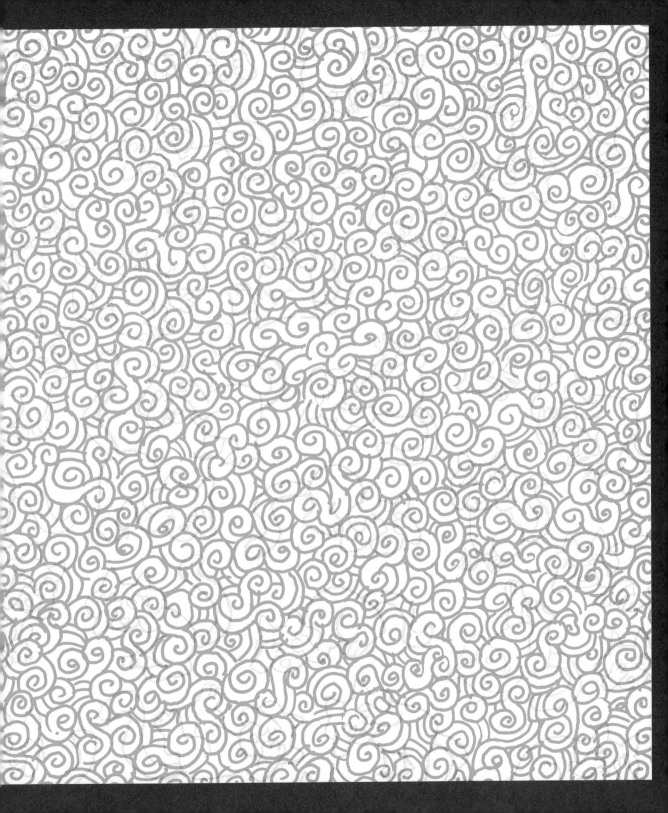

This elephant's talent

Is daring and slick,

When it comes to showing

His peek-a-boo trick.

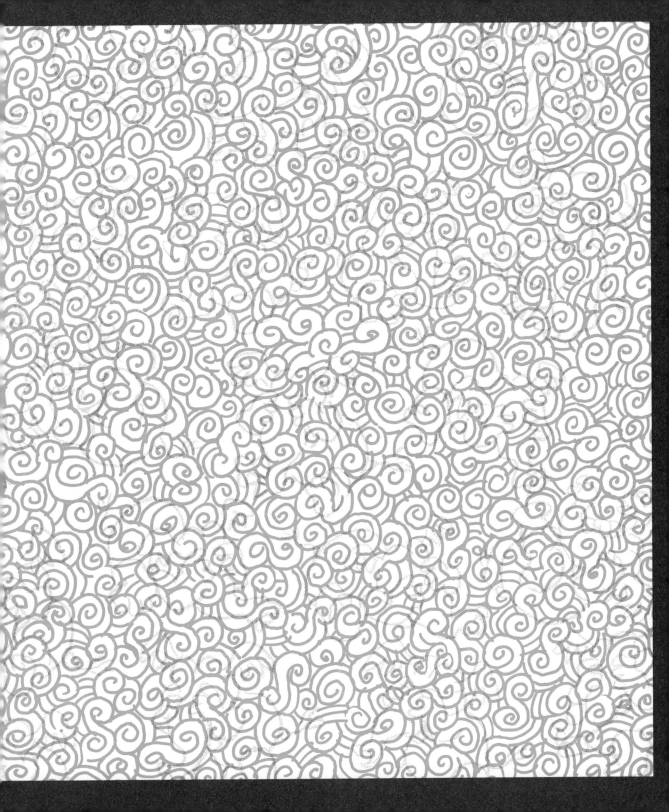

Count all your fingers,
Check your toes later,
And don't try to pet
A peek-a-boo 'gator.

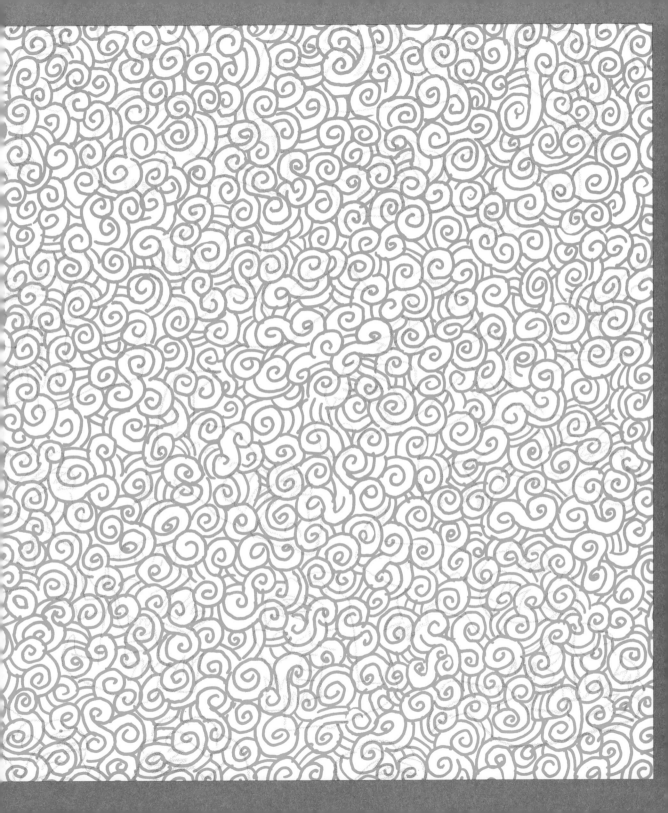

A curious monkey
Hanging from trees
Can peek-a-boo you
With the greatest of ease.

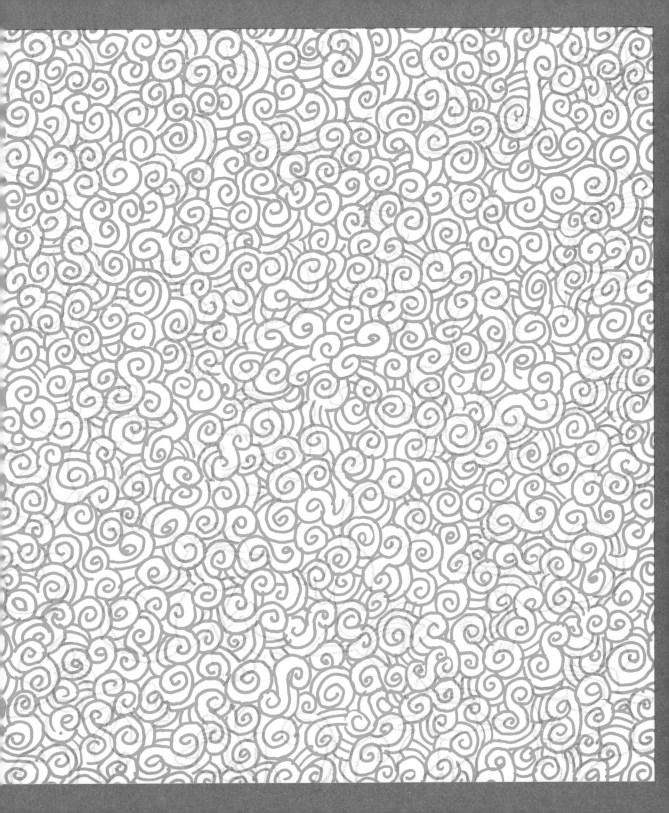

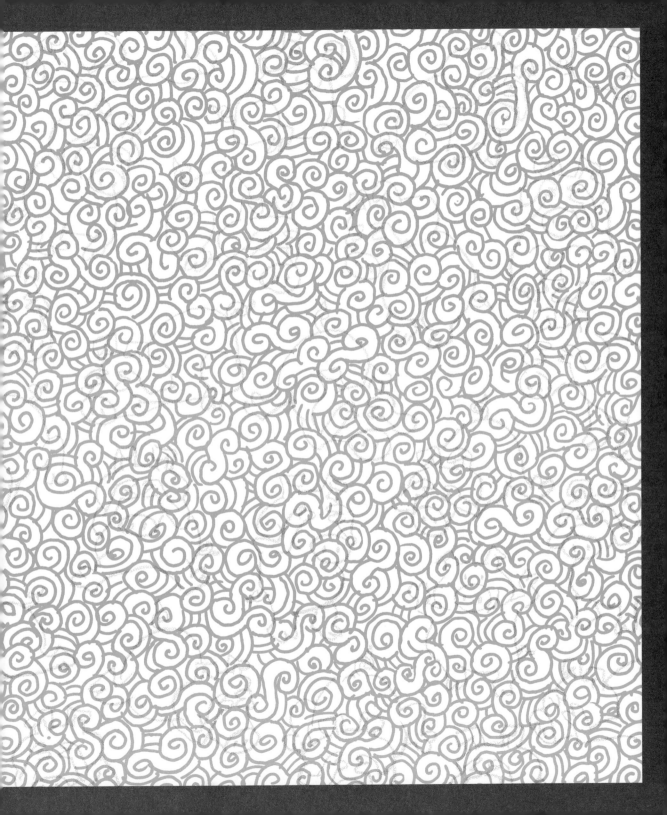

Hop and jump
And skip-to-my-Lou,
Can you find
A peek-a-boo roo?

Yawn and doze
And dream and sleep,
Can you count
A peek-a-boo sheep?

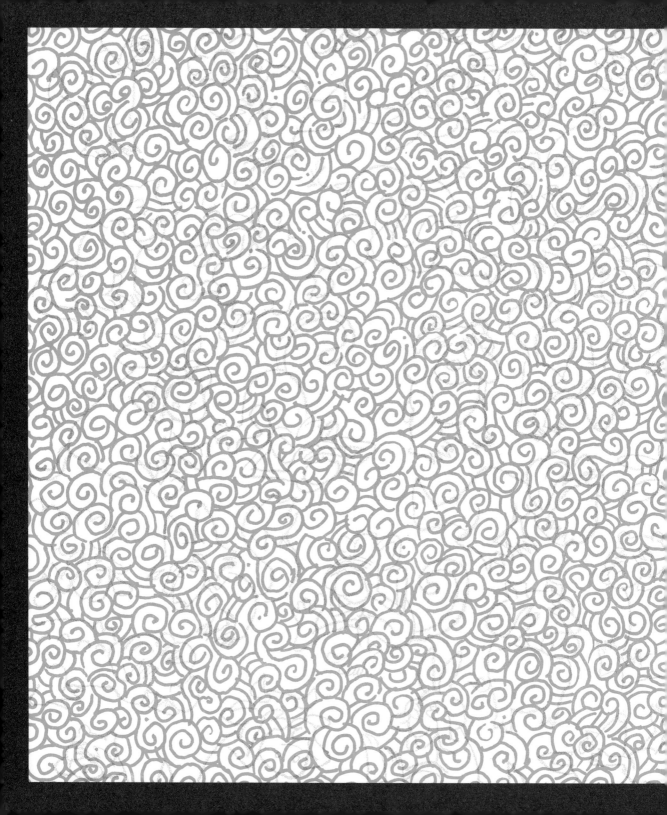

Fox's feet forward,
An elephant's behind,
This creature has parts
Of an unusual kind.

Horns of a cow
And a 'gator's big muzzle—
What beastie is this?
It's a peek-a-boo puzzle!

Did you find. . .

Peek-a-boo beast